Jim Arnosky

Rabbits & Raindrops

G. P. Putnam's Sons
New York

G. P. Putnam's Sons, a division of The Putnam & Grosset Group,
200 Madison Avenue, New York, NY 10016.
G. P. Putnam's Sons, Reg. U.S. Pat. & Tm. Off.
Published simultaneously in Canada.
Printed in Hong Kong by South China Printing Co. (1988) Ltd.
Book designed by Patrick Collins.
Text set in Horley Old Style.

Library of Congress Cataloging-in-Publication Data
Arnosky, Jim. Rabbits and raindrops / Jim Arnosky. p. cm.
Summary: Mother rabbit's five babies hop out of her nest to nibble clover,
meet grasshoppers, spiders, and bees, play tag, and run for shelter when it rains.
[1. Rabbits—Fiction.] I. Title.
PZ7.A7384Rad 1997 [E]—dc20 95-22921 CIP AC
ISBN 0-399-22635-4

1 3 5 7 9 10 8 6 4 2

First Impression

This book is dedicated to
Darren.

Mother rabbit sits
by her nest

under a hedge
at the edge
of green lawn.

Her five babies are ready
to climb out of the nest
for the first time.

Mother rabbit hops out
into the bright sunlight,

onto the green grass.

One after another,
the five baby rabbits
hop out onto the lawn.

They nibble clover
blossoms and leaves.

They meet grasshoppers,
spiders, and bees.

All of a sudden
the sky turns dark,
and big, heavy raindrops
begin to fall.

A rabbit's fur is not waterproof.
Baby rabbits can become
soaked, and catch cold.

So Mother rabbit hurries her babies back under the hedge.

From their dry shelter,
five baby rabbits
watch the rain pouring down.

A butterfly flutters in
under the hedge,
and rests on a dry leaf.

Soon others come inside,
out of the rain.

Out in the shower, honeybees buzz by,

flying between raindrops to stay dry.

Suddenly the shower ends,

and the last few raindrops splatter down.

All together, the rabbits hop
out onto the lawn . . .

. . . to taste the wet grass,
and play rabbit tag
in the sun.